Be Quiet, Bramble!

BENEDICT BLATHWAYT

For Jamie and Lucy

First published in 2021 by
BC Books
an imprint of
Birlinn Limited
West Newington House
10 Newington Road
Edinburgh EH9 1QS

www.bcbooksforkids.co.uk

ISBN: 978 1 78027 659 5

British Library Cataloguing-in-Publication Data
A catalogue record for this book is available
from the British Library

Designed by Mark Blackadder

Printed by PNB Print, Latvia

Bramble the cow lived on an old farm.
She had lots of friends and she was happy.

Sleeping peacefully beneath her favourite tree
was what Bramble liked best of all.

But Bramble did not like strange noises.
The angry buzzing of bees upset her.

A flock of ducks once woke Bramble up from her afternoon sleep.

She was so surprised she leapt over
the wall and into the pond!

She did not like the growl of the
farmer's combine harvester.

The farmer's bird-scaring gun
made Bramble jump.

She hated the scream of the jets
which flew low over the farm.

She was afraid of the roar of the wind.

The farmer knew Bramble hated storms.

He sometimes let her shelter in the barn until the storm was over.

But more than anything else, Bramble hated rain.
'You can't stay indoors whenever there's
a drop of rain!' laughed the farmer.

Bramble mooed and mooed whenever it rained.

One wet night, Bramble mooed all night long.
'Be quiet, Bramble!' shouted the farmer. 'We can't get any sleep.'

Bramble tried hard to be quiet, but it really was *very* wet.

In the morning, the farmer moved Bramble to a field far from
the farmhouse so they would not hear her mooing.

The sun came out at last and Bramble's friends
came down from the farm to see her.

'You must be quiet now, Bramble,' they said. 'It has stopped raining.'

Nobody noticed a big tree trunk floating
downstream towards the bridge.

The tree trunk blocked the river
and the field began to flood.

When Bramble and her friends saw
the flood they were frightened.

'Help!' squawked the hens.
'Hooray!' quacked the ducks.

The water got deeper very quickly.
'H…h…h…help!' bleated the sheep.
There was just enough room for the two of them on Bramble's back.

The water kept on rising. Bramble lifted her head and mooed
as loud as she could . . . again and again and again.

Far away, the farmer heard her.
'Be quiet, Bramble!' he shouted crossly.

But the mooing went on.

Suddenly, the farmer saw the flood – now he understood
why Bramble was making such a noise.

He rushed to fetch the rowing boat.
'I'm coming to get you!' he called.

But there wasn't room for Bramble in the boat.
She had to swim behind.

'Well done, Bramble!' said the farmer when
they reached dry land. 'What a hero!'

As a reward, the farmer let Bramble shelter in her
warm, dry shed whenever it rained heavily.